THE BEST CLASS PICTURE EVER!

DENIS ROCHE

SCHOLASTIC PRESS ☙ NEW YORK

It was Class Picture Day. As the second graders lined up, Olivia discovered that the class pet was missing.

"Elvis is gone!" she cried, and Class 202 fell into an uproar.

Quickly the search began. Shirts came untucked. Ties dropped off. Barrettes flew from heads.

The principal sighed. She hadn't been able to replace the teacher for Class 202, and now she knew why.

The room was turned upside-down, but Elvis was still missing.

"The photographer is waiting," said the principal. "We'll look for your guinea pig later." And off they went to the auditorium.

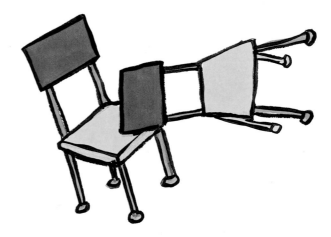

It had been another dull day for Mr. Click, the photographer. He had dozed off waiting for Class 202, but he was awakened suddenly by a commotion. Children rolled down the aisles, raced up the curtains, and kung fu kicked off the stage.

"Where's your teacher?" asked Mr. Click.

"We don't have one," said Norton and Carter together.

"It looks like you could use one," said Mr. Click, and he helped the twins re-tie their ties.

Mr. Click combed hair, reclipped barrettes, and double-knotted shoelaces. He arranged Class 202 on the benches and got ready to take their picture.

"Smile!" he said. Everybody smiled but Olivia.

"What's wrong?" asked Mr. Click.

"We don't have a teacher," howled Olivia. "And now we don't even have a class pet."

"I know just the thing to cheer you up," said Mr. Click.
He led Class 202 to a big mirror backstage.

"Look at your reflection and say 'cheese,'" he said. "See how it makes your mouth smile?"

"Cheeeeese. Cheeeeese. Cheeeeeeeeese," repeated Class 202. Everyone giggled. But not Olivia. She still couldn't smile.

Beth raised her hand.

"Maybe another word will help Olivia smile," she suggested.

"Let's make a list!" said Mr. Click, and he sent a monitor to get supplies.

Class 202 began their list.

underwear

trombone

banana

Louisiana

"'Hiccups'," suggested Norton. "Hiccups! Hiccups! Hiccups!"

Instead of smiling he began to hiccup uncontrollably.

"Hold your breath," said Olivia, and she smiled the tiniest of smiles.

" 'Feet' is a funny word," said Beth. "And so is 'toes.'"
Class 202 pulled off their shoes and socks to compare their feet and toes.

As Olivia helped Mr. Click get socks down from the lights,
her smile grew a little bit wider.

Mr. Click was pleased with Class 202's growing list. He handed out dictionaries so everything would be spelled correctly.

"'Moustache'!" cried Carter, holding a sock under his nose. "It's the same word in both English and French!" Olivia made a sock moustache, too, and smiled a bit more.

Class 202 now had a long list of words.
"How will we decide what word makes
Olivia smile biggest?" asked Norton.
"With rulers!" said Mr. Click.

underwear
trombone
banana
hiccups
feet
moustache
toes
walrus
pretzel
bobcat
Pekinese
tadpole
Louisiana
watchdog
snafu
Camembert
antelope
bicycle
mumble
purple
scatter
wallop
whiskers
goatee
belly-
button
barnacle
blue-
berry

banana

hiccups

underwear

Pekinese

"Hurrah!" said everyone. "'Trombone' wins!"

Just then, the principal returned. She couldn't believe how well-behaved Class 202 had become.

"How wonderful," she said when she saw their list. "You have done math and language skills! Better take that class picture though, it's getting late."

Class 202 sat on the benches.

"Trombo-o-o-o-one. Trombo-o-o-o-one. Trombo-o-o-o-o-o-one," they practiced. As Mr. Click was about to take the picture, something squeaked.

"Elvis!" cried Olivia, smiling ear to ear.

"Elvis!" cheered Class 202.

"Perfect!" said Mr. Click, and he took the picture.

On the way back to their classroom, Olivia had an idea.

She whispered it to the principal.

After lunch, Class 202 had a big surprise. They returned to
the auditorium and had another class picture taken. . . .

. . . And this time, nobody, not even Olivia, smiled bigger
than their new teacher, Mr. Click!